Disney · PIXAR

WALL·E

LEVEL 5

Re-told by: Helen Parker
Series Editor: Melanie Williams

Pearson Education Limited
Edinburgh Gate, Harlow,
Essex CM20 2JE, England
and Associated Companies throughout the world.

ISBN: 978-1-4082-8873-3

This edition first published by Pearson Education Ltd 2012

1 3 5 7 9 10 8 6 4 2

Set in 15/19pt OT Fiendstar
Printed in China
SWTC/01

Published by Pearson Education Ltd in association with
Penguin Books Ltd, both companies being subsidiaries of Pearson Plc

For a complete list of the titles available in the Penguin Kids series please go to www.penguinreaders.com.
Alternatively, write to your local Pearson Longman office or to: Penguin Readers Marketing Department,
Pearson Education, Edinburgh Gate, Harlow, Essex CM20 2JE, England.

A little robot called WALL-E moved through the mountains of trash on planet Earth.

The people escaped a long time ago when Earth became too dirty and dangerous. They all went to live on a big space station and left behind a lot of robots to clean the planet. Now WALL-E was the only robot on Earth.

Soon WALL-E arrived at his home – an old truck.

whoosh!

He heard the sound of a storm and he closed the door quickly.

WALL-E's home had pretty lights and shelves full of interesting things. He took out some things which he found in the trash that day. He put them carefully on the shelves. Then he watched his favorite movie. A man and a woman danced and held hands in the movie. WALL-E loved it and he watched it again and again.

He wanted to hold hands and dance like the people in the movie. But more than anything, he wanted a friend.

The next day, WALL-E went out to work. Every day, he put trash into his chest and squashed it to make neat cubes.

He often found interesting things in the trash. This time he found a lighter and an old boot. He put them into the case on his back.

Then he saw an old refrigerator ... He opened the door and found something small and green inside. He really liked the green thing. He put it carefully into the boot.

Just then WALL-E saw a strange red light at his feet. The light raced away and he ran after it. Then he saw a lot more red lights ...

Suddenly, there was a loud noise above him and WALL-E looked up. The lights were from a big spaceship. It nearly landed on WALL-E!

A big metal arm came out of the spaceship. The arm put something on the ground — it was white and round.

The spaceship took off and WALL-E hid behind a rock. The
white thing started to fly about like a bird. Sometimes it
stopped and scanned things with a blue light. It flew near to
WALL-E. Now he could see what it was – a female robot with
big blue eyes. She was very beautiful.

He moved to hide behind another rock, but he made a noise.
The robot turned and shot the rock with her arm.

Ka-boom!

WALL-E was scared, but he was okay. The white robot saw him at last. She flew toward him and scanned him with her blue light.

A little later she asked, "Name?" At first WALL-E did not understand, but then he answered, "Wwwaaallee!"

The white robot then said her name, "EVE."

"Eeevaah? Eee-vah! Eevah!" said WALL-E.

EVE laughed.

Suddenly, WALL-E heard the wind. It was another storm. WALL-E took EVE to his truck.

WALL-E showed EVE a lot of things in his truck. Then he showed her his favorite movie. She watched the people singing and dancing. WALL-E copied the dancing for EVE. He turned round and round. EVE tried to dance, too. She turned very fast and hit WALL-E!

SMASH!

She broke one of his eyes.

Everything was okay because WALL-E found a new eye on one of his shelves.

EVE picked up a lighter from the shelves. She held it up and WALL-E moved closer. She looked so beautiful in the light. WALL-E wanted to hold her hand, but he was too shy.

He wanted to find something interesting for EVE. Then he suddenly remembered the small green thing!

He held up the boot with the green thing inside. EVE looked very surprised to see a plant! Then something very strange happened ...

First, EVE scanned the plant with her blue light. Then two doors
in her chest opened and the light pulled the plant inside.

whoosh!

Next, her arms and head closed into her body. A green light
shone from her chest.

"Eevah!" WALL-E shouted, but she could not hear him. "Eevah!"
he called again, but EVE could not move. What could WALL-E
do to help his new friend?

WALL-E tried a lot of different things to wake her up. He took her for long walks. He sat with her for hours. Nothing worked.

The next day, WALL-E had to leave EVE and go to work. He just did his job and nothing more. He did not look for things in the trash. He could only think about EVE.

Suddenly, he heard a loud noise and saw a red light in the sky. Was it another storm?

No, it was not a storm — it was the big spaceship. A robot arm came out of the spaceship and picked up EVE.

WALL-E raced toward the spaceship. "Eevah! Eevah!" he cried, but he was too late.

Then the doors closed and WALL-E jumped onto the side of the spaceship. The spaceship took off and WALL-E held on with his small metal hands.

The spaceship flew by the moon, stars, and planets. It flew near Saturn and WALL-E touched its rings.

Soon he saw something big and white in front of him. It was the *Axiom* – the space station where the people from Earth now lived.

The spaceship landed on the *Axiom*. The doors opened and WALL-E saw some white robots with EVE. EVE was the only one with the green light.

A robot arm picked up EVE and put her on the *Axiom*. WALL-E sat with the other white robots and the arm picked him up, too.

Some little robots arrived. They cleaned the robots from the ship. A little robot called M-O tried to clean WALL-E. He looked very dirty!

A smaller robot called Gopher arrived. He was the Captain's robot. He scanned all the white robots. When he scanned EVE, an alarm started – it made a terrible noise!

Gopher jumped quickly into a truck and drove away with
EVE. WALL-E raced after them and M-O ran behind ... He still
wanted to clean WALL-E!

Soon they arrived on the deck of the *Axiom*. There were people
everywhere, but they were not like the people in WALL-E's
favorite movie ... They were much bigger, softer, and rounder.
They could not walk so they went everywhere in chairs. They all
had TV screens in front of their faces. They looked very bored.

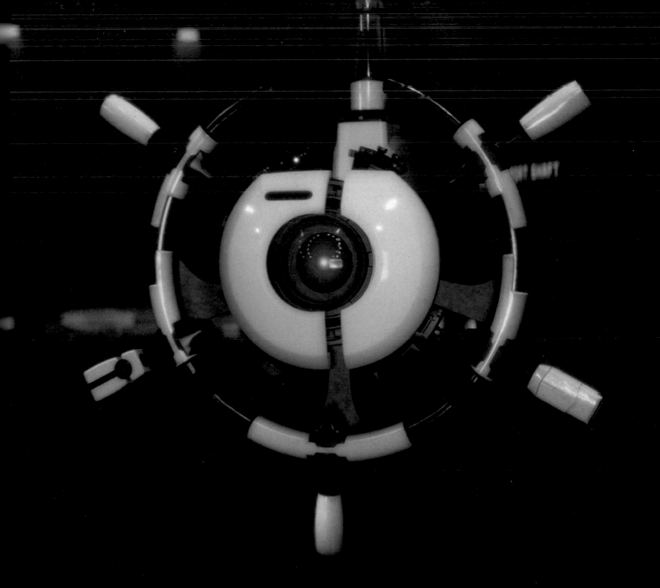

The truck arrived outside the Captain's room. The doors opened and Gopher drove inside. WALL-E followed the truck, then he hid in a corner.

In the center of the room was a big wheel. It was a robot called Auto and he was the *Axiom*'s pilot. He was there to help the Captain, but he decided everything.

Auto scanned EVE. A picture of a plant appeared on his computer screen. He had to call the Captain.

The Captain arrived. He looked at EVE and saw the picture of the plant on the computer screen. He pushed a big green button and a man appeared on the screen.

"Hello, Captain!" the man said, "I have fantastic news. If a plant can grow on Earth, people can live there, too. You can all go home! Just put the plant in the detector. The *Axiom* will take you home in no time!"

The Captain was excited. He wanted to see the plant and put it in the detector. The doors in EVE's chest opened, but there was no plant inside! WALL-E came out and looked everywhere for the plant.

Auto scanned EVE again, but he could not find anything. "This robot is broken," he told the Captain.

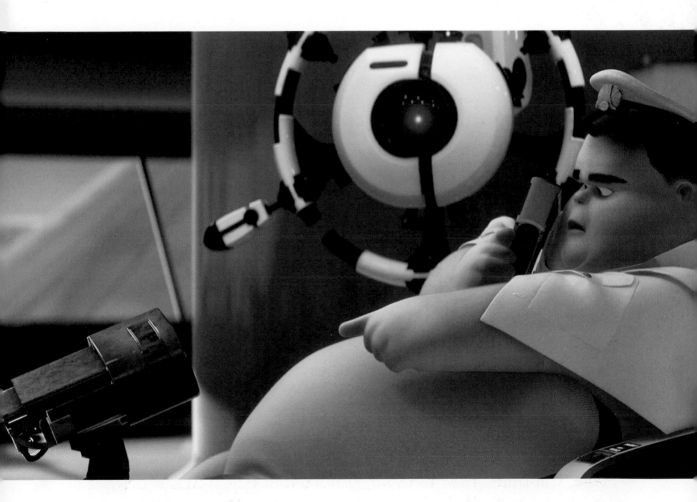

"Send her to the robot hospital," said the Captain. Then he pointed at WALL-E. "And clean this robot!"

WALL-E and EVE arrived at the robot hospital. It was full of sick and broken robots. A small pink robot jumped in front of WALL-E and painted his face. She held up a mirror. "Oh! You look so pretty!" she said.

They put WALL-E in a room next to a very sick robot. Then they put EVE in another room. They held her down and took off her arm.

WALL-E saw everything through the glass walls. He had to save her!

CRASH!

WALL-E broke through the glass and went into EVE's room.
He picked up her arm and shot into the air.

BANG! BANG!

Seconds later, lots of broken robots raced into the room. They
picked up WALL-E and carried him out of the hospital. EVE flew
after them ...

Suddenly, some police robots arrived. EVE flew down and picked
up WALL-E and her arm. The broken robots stopped the police
robots so EVE and WALL-E could escape!

EVE took WALL-E to a little rocket on the side of the *Axiom*. She wanted to save her friend. She pointed at the rocket and said, "Earth."

WALL-E went in and sat down. He pointed at the seat next to him. "Eevah?" he said softly.

EVE pointed at the green light in her chest. She had to stay and find the plant.

WALL-E raced out of the rocket. He did not want to go anywhere without EVE.

Just then, they heard a noise ... It was Gopher! WALL-E and EVE hid in the dark outside the little rocket. Gopher opened the doors in his chest and took out ... the plant! He put it in the rocket and came out. EVE was very surprised, but now she understood. It was Gopher who stole the plant!

She turned to WALL-E, but he was not there. He was in the rocket. He went to get the plant!

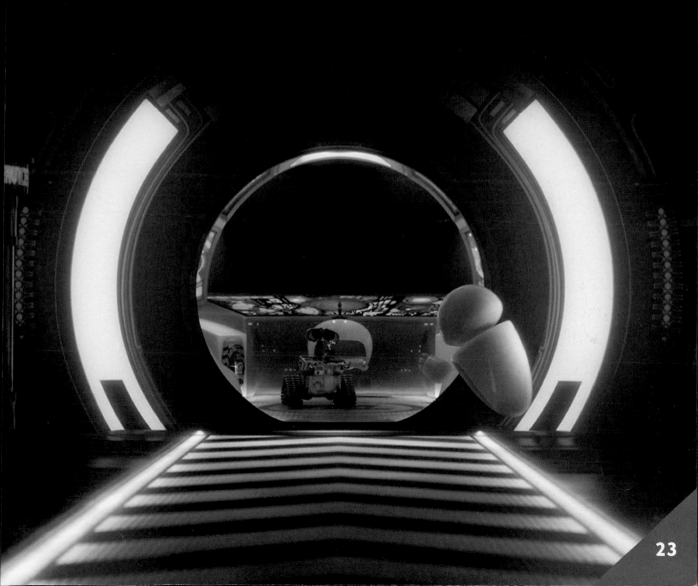

"WALL-E!" EVE shouted, but it was too late. Gopher pushed a button and the rocket took off with WALL-E and the plant! EVE jumped into another rocket and took off, too.

WALL-E was scared. He pushed a lot of buttons. Then he pushed the wrong button. "This rocket will explode in ten seconds," said a robot voice.

Ka-boom!

The rocket exploded and threw WALL-E into space.

EVE flew out of her rocket and caught WALL-E in her arms.

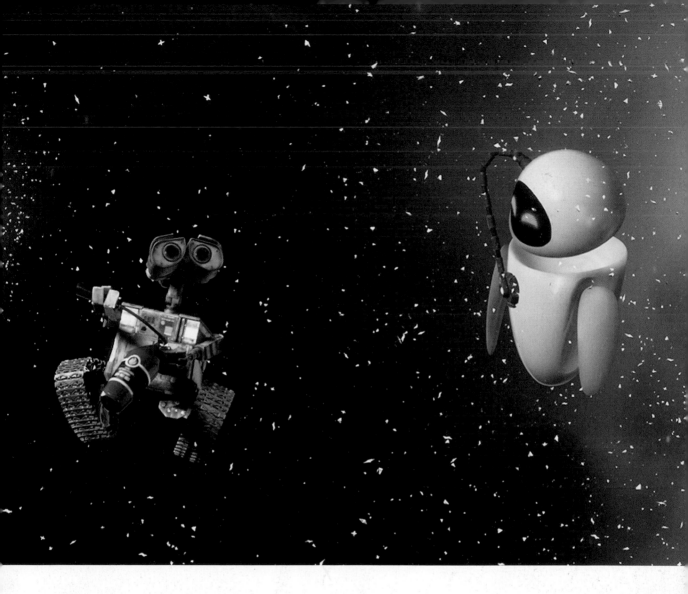

WALL-E and EVE danced together in space. Then WALL-E opened the door in his chest and showed the plant to EVE. She was so happy, she gave WALL-E a robot kiss!

Soon they were back on the *Axiom*. EVE wanted to take the plant to the Captain. She showed WALL-E a trash chute. It went up to the Captain's room.

EVE went into the chute and WALL-E waited for her.

EVE flew up the chute and took the plant to the Captain. He was surprised but very happy. "Turn on the plant detector!" he told Auto. "We're going home!"

"NO!" Auto shouted. "We are staying here! Give me the plant!"

"NO!" answered the Captain. "I am the Captain and we are going home *today*!"

Suddenly, Gopher raced into the room. He took the plant and threw it into the trash chute. Then he threw EVE into the chute, too!

WALL-E went to find EVE. He climbed up the chute ...

He caught the plant, but he could not catch EVE. They fell down the chute and landed in a mountain of trash. Some big robots picked up the trash and squashed it into cubes. WALL-E and EVE were in the cubes!

Quickly, EVE shot through the cube and escaped. Then she pulled WALL-E from his cube. He was badly broken, but he still had the plant!

In the Captain's room, Auto still did not want to turn on the detector. He did not want anything to change. He did not want to go back to Earth!

The Captain had an idea. Secretly, he turned on the computer and started to talk. His face appeared on every screen on the *Axiom*. "EVE ... the detector is near the swimming pool. Put the plant inside!"

Then, for the first time in his life, he stood up and walked toward Auto ...

The Captain fought bravely with Auto and won! He pushed the robot away and turned on the detector.

EVE flew with WALL-E to the swimming pool and put the plant in the detector.

Ten, nine, eight, seven, six ...

whoosh!

The *Axiom* landed on Earth and the doors opened.

The Captain and all the people looked at their true home. They stood up and walked slowly out of the *Axiom* to their new life.

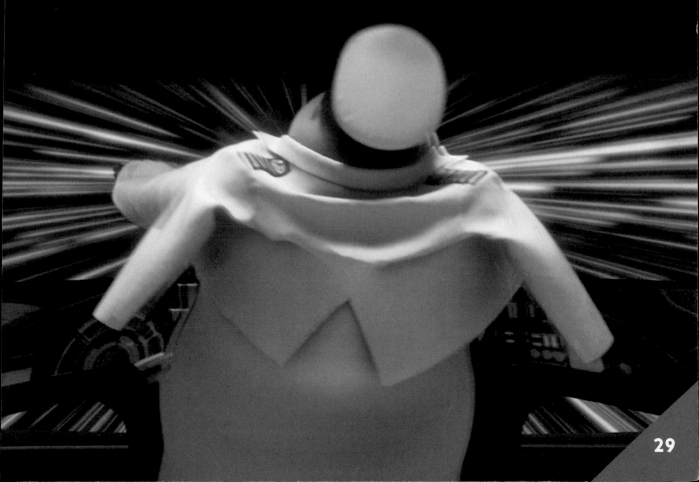

EVE flew with WALL-E to his truck and changed his broken parts.

WALL-E looked at EVE with his new eyes. At first he could not remember her.

But then she gave him a kiss and he remembered! "Eevah!" he said softly.

EVE held WALL-E's hand and looked into his eyes. She loved him and he loved her. At last WALL-E had everything he ever wanted.

Activity page ❶

Before You Read

❶ **Look at the picture on the front cover.**
Answer the questions.
  a What can you see?
  b Do you think it is male or female?
  c What is its name?
  d What does it look like?

❷ **Now look at the pictures in the book. Find these things.**
Write the page number(s) in your notebook.
  a a plant in a boot
  b a cube of trash
  c a lighter
  d a small white robot
  e a robot holding the outside of a spaceship
  f a fat man in a chair
  g the captain of the space station
  h a pink robot
  i a big wheel

Activity page 2

After You Read

1 **Put the sentences in the right order.**

   a The *Axiom* landed on Earth.

   b EVE put the plant in her body.

   c The Captain sent EVE and WALL-E to the hospital.

   d WALL-E found a plant in a refrigerator.

   e EVE and WALL-E put the plant in the detector.

   f EVE and WALL-E landed on the *Axiom*.

   g The Captain fought Auto and won!

   h WALL-E took off in a small rocket which exploded!

   i WALL-E and EVE landed in a mountain of trash.

   j The Captain appeared on every screen on the *Axiom*.

2 **Correct the sentences.**

   a The people left Earth and went to live on another planet.

   b Robots danced in WALL-E's favorite movie.

   c EVE broke WALL-E's arm when she danced.

   d Gopher tried to clean WALL-E.

   e The people on the *Axiom* were very thin.

   f The plant detector was next to the hospital.

   g Auto stole the plant from EVE when she arrived.

   h When the *Axiom* landed on Earth, the Captain stayed in the spaceship.

3 **Which is your favorite part of the story? Why? Draw a picture from this part of the story. Talk about it with your class.**